START YOUR ENGINES!

# MONSTER TRUCKS

By Martha London

**Kaleidoscope**
Minneapolis, MN

## The Quest for Discovery Never Ends

...............................................

This edition first published in 2020 by Kaleidoscope Publishing, Inc.

No part of this publication may be reproduced in whole or in part without written permission of the publisher.

For information regarding permission, write to
Kaleidoscope Publishing, Inc.
6012 Blue Circle Drive
Minnetonka, MN 55343

Library of Congress Control Number
2019940181

ISBN
978-1-64519-059-2 (library bound)
978-1-64494-217-8 (paperback)
978-1-64519-160-5 (ebook)

Text copyright © 2020 by Kaleidoscope Publishing, Inc. All-Star Sports, Bigfoot Books, and associated logos are trademarks and/or registered trademarks of Kaleidoscope Publishing, Inc.

Printed in the United States of America.

**FIND ME IF YOU CAN!**

Bigfoot lurks within one of the images in this book. It's up to you to find him!

# TABLE OF **CONTENTS**

**Chapter 1: Monster Jam** ............................................................. **4**

**Chapter 2: Built for Crushing** ................................................. **10**

**Chapter 3: Bigger and Better** ................................................ **16**

**Chapter 4: Rally Time** ............................................................ **22**

    Beyond the Book ............................................................ 28
    Research Ninja ................................................................ 29
    Further Resources .......................................................... 30
    Glossary ............................................................................ 31
    Index ................................................................................. 32
    Photo Credits .................................................................. 32
    About the Author ........................................................... 32

### CHAPTER 1

# Monster Jam

Toni and her parents sit in the stadium. People pile into the building. They stream down the stairs to their seats. The stands are crowded. Everyone is excited for the show to start.

Loud music thumps through the speakers. A man walks up and down the steps. He carries a tray of hot dogs and soda. He yells and people raise their hands. Toni's mom orders hot dogs. But all Toni smells is gasoline.

Toni was here was for a football game once. The ground was covered in fake grass then. Tonight, dirt and sand fill the floor. Ramps sit in the middle. Monster trucks will use them during the show. They'll launch off the jumps.

For monster truck rallies, stadiums are set up with jumps, ramps, and other obstacles.

Suddenly, the music cuts out. An announcer comes over the speakers. He shouts, "Are you ready?" His voice echoes in the huge stadium. It is very loud. Toni feels the sound vibrate through her. The crowd cheers.

Then she hears the trucks. The drivers rev their engines. They are still out of sight. Everyone waits for the trucks to come out. Toni loves the excitement.

Monster trucks often make exciting, dramatic entrances when they're introduced at rallies.

The first truck roars as it enters the arena. It is yellow. The tires have huge ridges on them. These grooves grip the dirt. The truck speeds around curves. It slides in the sand.

*The monster truck Megalodon is a favorite at monster truck rallies.*

Toni always knew monster trucks were big. But this is the first time she's seen them in person. She's high up in the stands. But the trucks still look massive.

The trucks enter one by one. Toni's favorite is Megalodon. It looks like a huge shark. It even has a shark tail on the back. Megalodon charges at the ramp. It flies through the air. Toni holds her breath as Megalodon lands. The truck bounces as it turns. It nearly flips over. But it stays right side up. The crowd goes wild!

**CHAPTER 2**

# Built for Crushing

Bob Chandler had a 1974 Ford F-250. His friends called him "Bigfoot" because he liked to go fast. Chandler painted that name on his Ford. It fit the huge truck. Chandler kept putting bigger tires and **axles** on his truck. He took it to mudding competitions. But that wasn't enough.

Bigfoot the truck became a character. It was different. It was huge. At first, Chandler just raced around arenas. People cheered. They loved watching the dirt spray behind the wheels.

*Bigfoot started out going to mudding competitions and racing around arenas.*

# MONSTER TRUCK
## STATS

| ENGINE | TRANSMISSION |
|---|---|
| V8 | Automatic |
| **BASE PRICE** | **WEIGHT** |
| $250,000 | 10,000–12,000 pounds (4,500–5,400 kg) |
| **HORSEPOWER** | **SPECIAL FEATURES** |
| 1,500 horsepower | Specialized suspension, oversized tires, custom paint |

Bigfoot appeared at an event near Detroit, Michigan. An organizer called Bigfoot a "monster truck." The name stuck. *Monster truck* started describing this type of vehicle.

Chandler wanted to see what his truck could do. He drove it onto a car. A promoter saw a video of this. He wanted Chandler to do it in front of a crowd. Chandler headed to Missouri.

Bigfoot rolled over a car. The metal beneath the truck creaked and cracked. The audience whooped and hollered. They loved it. They wanted to see more car-crushing action.

**FUN FACT**
A different monster truck, King Kong, may have actually been the first truck to crush a car.

Monster trucks driving over and crushing cars is a big part of rallies today.

**FUN FACT**
Bigfoot 5's tires were 10 feet (3 m) tall!

*Many different versions of the Bigfoot monster truck have been made over the years.*

Soon, lines of junk cars sat in arenas. Monster truck tires smashed windows and doors. Drivers raced each other over the cars. Then they launched their trucks over the cars. They wanted to see what their trucks could handle.

Chandler was always trying to improve his trucks. He made different versions of Bigfoot. Today, monster trucks are a big deal. They're a billion-dollar business in the United States. The original Bigfoot appears at car shows and rallies. But it isn't crushing any more cars.

## FLYING OVER A JET PLANE

In 1999, Bigfoot 14 tried something new. It was going to jump over a 727 jet plane. No other monster truck had done it. Dan Runte was the driver. He sped toward the ramp. Bigfoot flew high into the air. It flew 202 feet (62 m). Bigfoot landed on the other side of the plane!

**CHAPTER 3**

# Bigger and Better

The tires are off. The **fiberglass** shell stands in a corner. The shell covers the **roll cage**. It makes Tara's monster truck look like a regular truck. But many details are just stickers. Tara needs to check the frame. She was in a rally last week. She rolled her monster truck. She has to make sure the frame isn't damaged.

Tara has extra pipes to replace her roll cage. Spare axles are on hand for when her truck's axles crack. She also has new **shocks** that she wants to try out. Tara loves doing jumps in her truck. She flies off the ramp and high into the air. The truck lands hard on the ground. There's no pillow to cushion its fall. The shocks will soften the blow.

*During rallies, monster trucks can get damaged from crashing or rolling.*

**FUN FACT**
The average monster truck needs eight new tires every year.

Monster trucks have many modifications to their suspension systems to help them absorb impact and stay steady.

Tara loves **modifying** her monster truck. She started working on cars in high school. Tara had always liked monster trucks. She found an old Chevy in the junkyard. Tara and her uncle used a **lift kit** on the truck. It needed to be raised high off the ground. Larger tires would fit on it that way. Huge tires are what make monster trucks monsters.

Tara learned the suspension was important. Better shock absorption put less stress on the truck's axles.

## ZOOM IN ON A
# MONSTER TRUCK

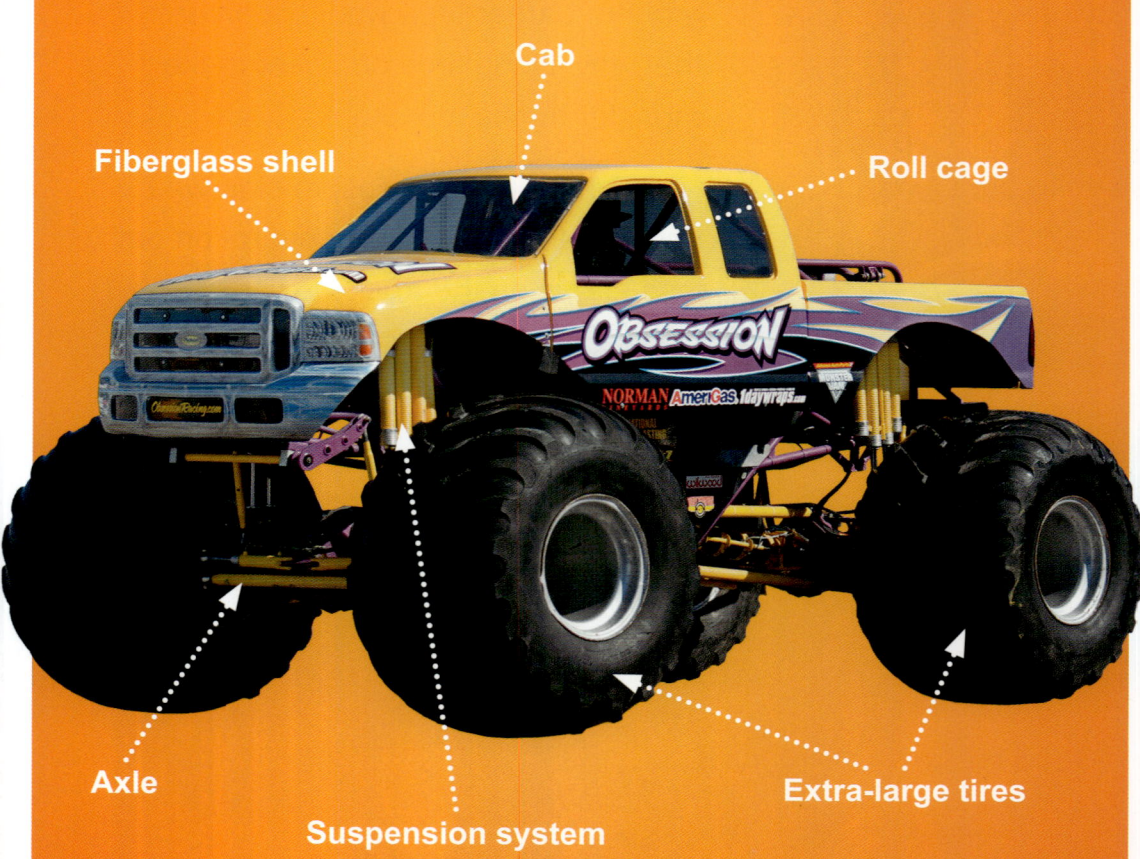

Cab

Fiberglass shell

Roll cage

Axle

Suspension system

Extra-large tires

Tara takes an electric wrench. The tool whirs in her hand. She unscrews the old shocks from the axle. Grease and dirt cover her hands. The shocks look worn. No wonder her truck has felt bumpier than usual. The new shocks will give it a smoother ride. She can't wait to test them out at the next rally.

*Rough landings can put a lot of strain on a monster truck's suspension system.*

# CHAPTER 4

# Rally Time

The inside of the monster truck is bare. Metal rods surround Eli. They're part of the roll cage. Over the frame is the shell. It's painted to look like a normal truck. But there aren't headlights. There aren't even doors.

Eli hears the motor roar behind him. Regular truck engines are in the front. But that would make a monster truck's nose too heavy. Monster trucks have rear engines. This helps balance the truck. It's less likely to flip over after a jump.

Eli checks his helmet. He adjusts his neck collar. Gloves cover his hands. He is strapped into his racing seat. Its extra straps keep him safe. Eli looks around the arena. People in the stands wave flags and posters.

*For safety, monster trucks have rear engines and their drivers wear protective gear.*

Officials test emergency off switches. Eli could lose control of the truck. The officials can help him if that happens. They can shut the truck off with a remote control.

Monster truck rallies feature freestyle, racing, and many other events.

Soon, the freestyle event begins. It's Eli's favorite part of monster truck rallies. He can do whatever he wants. He uses the jumps and the junk cars. He spins in the dirt. Crowds fill the seats of the stadium. Eli can hear them cheer over the loud engine. They chant his car's name: "Beast! Beast! Beast!"

He puts his foot to the pedal. The monster truck revs. It leaps forward. Eli steers the truck over one of the ramps. He flies through the air. His truck bounces hard on the landing. Next, Eli spins his truck in a circle. He sends up a fog of dirt and dust. He takes a lap around the arena. People stand and wave. Judges give him a score for creativity. But it's not about the points to Eli. He just loves making fans happy.

# HOW BIG IS A MONSTER TRUCK?

**FUN FACT**
About 3,000 cars are crushed at monster truck events every year.

Width
12.5 feet (3.8 m)

## PICKUP TRUCK

Width
7 feet (2.1 m)

Length
17 feet (5.2 m)

# MONSTER TRUCK

Height
10.5 feet
(3.2 m)

Tire Height
5.5 feet
(1.7 m)

Length
17.5 feet (5.3 m)

Height
6 feet
(1.8 m)

Tire Height
2.5 feet
(0.75 m)

# BEYOND THE BOOK

After reading the book, it's time to think about what you learned. Try the following exercises to jumpstart your ideas.

## THINK

**THAT'S NEWS TO ME.** In 1999, Bigfoot 14 flew over a jet plane. Consider how news sources might be able to fill in more details on the event. What new information could be found in news articles? Where could you go to find those news sources?

## CREATE

**SHARPEN YOUR RESEARCH SKILLS.** Drivers wear protective gear like helmets and neck collars when they drive monster trucks. Where could you go in the library, or who could you talk to, to find more information on monster truck safety? Create a research plan by writing a paragraph that details these next steps for research.

## SHARE

**SUM IT UP.** Write a paragraph summarizing the important points from the whole book. Write the summary in your own words—don't just copy from the text. Then share your summary with a classmate. Does your classmate have any feedback on the summary or additional questions about monster trucks?

## GROW

**DRAWING CONNECTIONS.** Create a diagram that shows and explains the connections between monster trucks and suspension systems. How does learning about suspension systems help you better understand monster trucks?

# RESEARCH NINJA

Visit *www.ninjaresearcher.com/0592* to learn how to take your research skills and book report writing to the next level!

## RESEARCH

**DIGITAL LITERACY TOOLS**

**SEARCH LIKE A PRO**
Learn about how to use search engines to find useful websites.

**FACT OR FAKE?**
Discover how you can tell a trusted website from an untrustworthy resource.

**TEXT DETECTIVE**
Explore how to zero in on the information you need most.

**SHOW YOUR WORK**
Research responsibly—learn how to cite sources.

## WRITE

**GET TO THE POINT**
Learn how to express your main ideas.

**PLAN OF ATTACK**
Learn prewriting exercises and create an outline.

**DOWNLOADABLE REPORT FORMS**

# Further Resources

**BOOKS**

Abdo, Kenny. *Monster Truck Rallies*. Abdo, 2019.

Adamson, Thomas K. *Monster Trucks*. Bellwether Media, 2019.

Ransom, Candice. *Monster Trucks*. North Star Editions, 2017.

**WEBSITES**

Factsurfer.com gives you a safe, fun way to find more information.

1. Go to www.factsurfer.com.
2. Enter "Monster Trucks" into the search box and click 🔍.
3. Select your book cover to see a list of related websites.

# Glossary

**axles:** Axles are metal rods that hold the wheels in place. Monster truck axles can crack after a hard landing.

**fiberglass:** Fiberglass is a hard plastic material that is used for racing vehicles. Monster trucks have a fiberglass shell over the frame.

**horsepower:** Horsepower is a unit of power that measures how much work is being done and how quickly it is being done. Monster truck engines have very high horsepower.

**lift kit:** A lift kit is used to raise a vehicle off the ground by replacing the suspension and supporting the vehicle's added height. Tara and her uncle used a lift kit to increase the truck's ground clearance.

**modifying:** If someone is modifying something, they are changing it. Tara is modifying her monster truck by putting different shocks on it.

**roll cage:** A roll cage is a metal frame in a vehicle that protects the driver if the vehicle flips over. Tara was thankful for her roll cage when her monster truck rolled over during a rally.

**shocks:** Shocks absorb impact from bumps on a track or road. Monster trucks have huge shocks to take the pressure off the axles after a jump.

**suspension:** The suspension system in a truck connects its shocks and axles and cushions it from the impact of rough roads or tracks. Monster trucks have strong suspension systems.

# Index

axles, 10, 16, 19, 20, 21

Bigfoot, 10, 12, 14, 15

Chandler, Bob, 10, 12, 15

crushing cars, 12, 13, 15, 26

dirt, 4, 7, 10, 21, 25

emergencies, 23

engines, 6, 11, 22, 25

Ford F-250, 10

freestyle, 25

jumps, 4, 15, 16, 22, 25

King Kong, 13

Megalodon, 9

ramps, 4, 9, 15, 16, 25

repairs, 16–21

roll cage, 16, 20, 22

Runte, Dan, 15

shells, 16, 20, 22

size, 11, 26–27

stadiums, 4, 6, 22, 25

suspension, 11, 19, 20, 21

tires, 7, 10, 11, 14, 15, 16, 18, 19, 20

## PHOTO CREDITS

The images in this book are reproduced through the courtesy of: Nigel Jarvis/Shutterstock Images, front cover; Natursports/Shutterstock Images, pp. 3, 30; BW Press/Shutterstock Images, pp. 4–5, 8–9, 9, 16–17, 22–23, 25; EvrenKalinbacak/Shutterstock Images, pp. 6–7; Barry Salmons/Shutterstock Images, p. 7; Bogdan Denysyuk/Shutterstock Images, p. 10; Red Line Editorial, p. 11 (chart); Amra Pasic/Shutterstock Images, p. 11 (truck); Michael Stokes/Shutterstock Images, pp. 12–13; Maksim Shmeljov/Shutterstock Images, pp. 14–15, 21; Joe_Potato/iStockphoto, p. 16; Simon Bratt/Shutterstock Images, pp. 18–19; Photomarine/Shutterstock Images, p. 19; Gunter Nezhoda/Shutterstock Images, p. 20; Piotr Zajac/Shutterstock Images, pp. 24–25; Mishella/Shutterstock Images, pp. 26–27 (monster truck); nitinut380/Shutterstock Images, pp. 26–27 (pickup truck).

## ABOUT THE AUTHOR

Martha London lives in Saint Paul, Minnesota. She writes children's books full-time. When she isn't writing, you can find her hiking in the woods.